MORGAN

Lesley Cox

MORGAN
Copyright © 2023 by Lesley Cox

Library of Congress Control Number: 2023905992
ISBN-13: Paperback: 978-1-64749-901-3

All rights reserved. No part of this publication may be reproduced, distributed, or transmitted in any form or by any means, including photocopying, recording, or other electronic or mechanical methods, without the prior written permission of the publisher or author, except in the case of brief quotations embodied in critical reviews and certain other noncommercial uses permitted by copyright law.

Although every precaution has been taken to verify the accuracy of the information contained herein, the author and publisher assume no responsibility for any errors or omissions. No liability is assumed for damages that may result from the use of information contained within.

Printed in the United States of America

GoToPublish LLC
1-888-337-1724
www.gotopublish.com
info@gotopublish.com

TABLE OF CONTENTS

Section 1 1
Section 2 5
Section 3 7
Section 4 11
Section 5 15
Section 6 17
Section 7 19
Section 8 25
Section 9 31
Section 10 39
Section 11 43

This book is dedicated to my brother, Butch Chase. I wish you were still here Bro.

My adopted family in Alaska, Lynda and Deanie Kaviskanov, my husband for his faith in me, Michael.

I love you all.

SECTION 1

Stacy is pacing back and forth between the house and the point overlooking the marina. There is still no sign of her husband or his boat. She is half way back to the point as the phone rings in the house. She races for the phone and grabs it just as it goes dead. At her wits end, she decides to call the authorities as it has become unbearable waiting and there is just enough daylight left for them to do a search. She also calls her friends to cancel the dinner party that was planned for that night. They all say they will come and wait with her but she begs them not to. She has to wait alone; at least for a while. The Coast Guard is called and given the details and they begin a search for her husband's boat. The sheriff waits with Stacy and there are several marked police cars in the drive when her friends arrive against her wishes. With them there, she feels that she has to put on a facade and not appear near to hysteria. The murmur of voices is heard throughout the house and Stacey just paces. Phones ring but others answer and she continues to pace. It is full dark now and nothing has been found of the boat or her husband.

The sheriff takes her into the den and asks all of the usual questions. Were they happy in their marriage? Did her husband have a girlfriend? Did they have money trouble? Did he have an insurance policy? Stacey answers his questions without anger because she knew this was just standard procedure. Yes, their marriage was happy. No, her husband had no girlfriend. No, they were comfortable and well off financially. Of course her husband had an insurance policy. After all, he was a responsible man with a wife. It would be suspicious if he did not have an insurance policy. The sheriff wanted to know how big a policy and was there double indemnity for accidental death. The policy was for one million dollars and yes, double indemnity for accidental death.

After a few more questions, it was decided to wait until morning. After all, her husband was a very good sailor and it was possible that he had been forced to pull into shore somewhere along the way if there was a problem with the boat. Surely by morning they would hear and the Coast Guard would resume their search. Everyone left telling Stacey that she was to call them if she needed anything at all. She smiled and thanked them but in her heart and head she was screaming. After the tail lights of the car disappeared around the corner she let out a huge breath of relief. Alone at last, she thought that they would never leave. She didn't have a lot of time because she knew that at first light they would all be back so she ran to the bedroom and pulled the suitcases that were already packed from the closet and took them to the garage. All of the contents were new and had been purchased over a period of time at discount stores. Places where no one would ever suspect that Stacey would shop. She disturbed nothing in the house. She didn't move one object and left the glasses and coffee cups in the sink, as they had been when everyone had left. She left her purse where it always was on the table by the front door. She had another purse with new identification and plenty of money in it. Enough money to go anywhere she wanted and to do anything she liked. She looked the house over for any signs of movement and found none. The bed was made up as it always was. Everything was in its place. She laid her nightgown over the chair by the bed and hung a damp towel over the towel rod in the bathroom as if she had showered before going to bed. It was only around 1 a.m. and she was going to wait until 3 to leave so she walked down to the point again and stood looking out into the darkness towards the light in the marina. She could see the light at the slip where her husband kept his beloved boat but she knew that neither he nor his boat would ever come into that slip again. She turned to walk back to the house only after taking her shoes off and walking on the shale that bordered the point. She approached the house from another direction leaving no footprints behind.

A little before 3 am, she turned out some of the lights and left others burning. She walked over to the garage and picked up her suitcases and went on into the woods near the house, again walking on the shale drive. Going into the woods for a short way, she found the car that she had hidden there. It had been so easy to hide because the woods were thick and she had parked it in such a way as not to be seen from the house or the road. It was dark in color and blended in with the trees. She loaded the luggage and left the drive with the lights off. There was no trace of the car or of Stacey. It was as if she had vanished into thin air. The last trace of her was at the edge of the point overlooking the marina. At the drive she turned to the left towards the mountains rather than right toward the town.

Stacey didn't drive far. She drove until the sky began to lighten and pulled into a motel that looked clean but unobtrusive. She had already made the arrangements for a room towards the back and off of the side that faced the road. Leaving everything in the car except for a small overnight bag and her purse, she went into town. She is sure that the realtor and those in the town many miles away have forgotten all about her and the cabin.

After she first bought it, she would make secret trips to what became known to her as her "hideout". She hired local schoolboys to do the work around the place that had to be done. She herself did the inside work and it is just as she dreamed it would be. Her husband was away so often on business that it was easy to bring things that she would need up here and stock the cabin. She has a wood-burning stove and again the local schoolboys have filled the shed outside with cut wood for the winter. She had brought staples with her on the last trip so all she needs now are perishables. She parked her little car in the garage that was attached to the shed that led to the main cabin by a breezeway made of fir branches. It was easy to get the car unloaded and her things in the cabin.

No one knew she was here and she intended to keep it that way for as long as possible. She would not mix and mingle with the people of the town. She intended to wait here until what she came for happened. She had no idea how long that would be but she knew that she couldn't leave.

From the time Stacey left her home by the sea, she had been wearing blue jeans and a blue denim shirt with sneakers and a zip up jacket. Her hair had been hidden under a baseball cap. She wore no make-up or jewelry, doesn't own a pair of jeans, and had put on glasses with clear glass in them, as she didn't need glasses. Once inside the rented motel room, she locked the door, laid down on the bed, and was instantly asleep.

At dawn she woke and was ready to continue her journey. She was completely calm and serene while knowing that she should be upset and frantic. She knew her husband was dead and that his boat was destroyed. Their marriage had been a good one even though they had never been able to have children. She loved him but she knew that she had to leave. There was nothing to go back to and something had been drawing her away from her home for such a long time. Thus, all of the arrangements to leave made in advance. She would have had to leave whether her husband was alive or dead. She had no choice in the matter, as it was something that she knew she had to do. After a quick cup of coffee at a diner, she pushes the little car higher and higher into the mountains.

SECTION 2

Stacey drives all day and enjoys the beautiful view as she gets higher and can look down into the valley below. She isn't hungry and has filled a thermos with coffee so she just keeps driving. Come nightfall she finds another small motel where she can sleep for a few hours before moving on. After a shower, she again falls asleep instantly.

Stacey has not had the radio on, nor has she read the newspaper, so she has no idea what has happened back at the house that she has called home for so many years. It is true that her husband has not been found, however, her disappearance has. All of the clues point to Stacey falling over the cliff at the point of the property and being carried out to sea. There is no indication anywhere that foul play was involved and no clue that she left of her own accord. It is assumed that in her grief she lost her footing and fell. However, the search for her husband continues and will until it is accepted that he too is lost forever.

Stacey awakens early, before the sun is up and is refreshed and ready to go. She again leaves in her little car so happy to have it. It is cozy and is easy to maneuver along the mountain roads. Toward dusk she turns into a dirt road. After about six feet, she has to stop the car and get out to open an old rusted gate. She drives through and closes the gate behind her. It is starting to rain so she knows that any tracks of her turning off of the main road will soon be gone. She drives slowly because the road isn't a good one. It is dirt and filled with rocks and potholes. As she makes the last turn she sees the cabin. Stacy doesn't know why but she knows that when she started making these arrangements so long ago there was a reason and she was not permitted to go back. The cabin and all of the land surrounding it belong to her. It is all paid for and has been for several years. It is so isolated that few people even know it exists and those that do think it is abandoned.

Nobody comes this way because it is said that the cabin is falling down and there isn't anything here to steal. Stacey knows better as she was lead here several years ago by intuition. She paid cash for the land with the story to the realtor that she was going to fix the place up for her retirement. It has been such a long time since her denim shirt or sneakers or any of the other clothes she was wearing. She had bought all of them at the discount store. Nobody who knew Stacey would ever guess that she would wear such an outfit. She had always dressed with class. Wearing chinos or wrap skirts and flats or sandals. She always wore jewelry, not a lot but some. Her wedding ring of course and usually pearls in her ears and perhaps a bracelet at times. She was ultra conservative and dressed the part that she had to play for her husband's business. All of that had been left behind except for the wedding ring. It would have raised suspicion if it had been left behind, as she never took it off. She now took it off and put it into a small pouch and laid it in the dresser drawer in the small bedroom.

SECTION 3

Stacy had the wherewithal to have the cabin upgraded without anyone knowing about it except the people who brought things from other towns. After such a long time, anyone with any questions would think that the lady had bought the cabin and then, for whatever reason decided not to use it. It had a large living area with the open kitchen separated by a bar. There was one bedroom and one bathroom. Off of the kitchen, there was a small utility room that had a clothes washer and dryer along with a hot water heater. There was no television or radio but there was a portable CD player because she loved music. That had been the biggest of the boxes she transported. Her music collection and her books, as books were her passion. She had made arrangements for additional books and music to be sent to a post office box in the town half a day's drive away from her cabin so that she could continue to read and listen to music. She had hoped that she would only have to make the trip once every other week or so.

The kitchen was well equipped, as Stacey was an excellent cook and liked to eat good food. The main room had hardwood floors with colorful throw rugs here and there. Right in front of the wood stove was a couch with a very comfortable chair and table in between. There were several small tables around the room and shelves where she could store her books. The bedroom was simply furnished. There was a double bed with a bedside table on one side. A dresser and chest of drawers took up one wall and another chair with an ottoman by the window. The bedroom was large enough to have had more furniture, but Stacey didn't want to fill the room to overflowing. The bed had a lovely chenille bedspread and there were throw pillows on the bed as well as the chair. There were also throw rugs in the bedroom and it was very colorful and cozy at the same time. There was a smaller wood stove in the bedroom and wood piled high in a basket sat by the stove. The bath had a claw-footed tub, sink, toilet and a table under the window where she planned to put a plant. She also loved plants and flowers surrounding her. The only other room in the cabin was a living room at the front of the house. This room was unfurnished, as it would not be used. It remained dark and no one from the outside would be able to tell that the cabin was indeed inhabited. She didn't need or want extravagant but she did want comfort.

The only outside help she had was electricity. She needed no phone nor gas and her water came from a well. The electric bill would be paid immediately out of an account set up at a bank far enough away that there would be no suspicion. It was sent to the bank for a draw and the bank would pay it. That and the bills for the books and music that she collected would be the only bills, and the bank would take care of them without knowing or caring who or what she was. They didn't know who she was because she had changed her name and had new identification, so everything that came to her would be under the new name. Anything else she needed, she would pay for in cash and she had enough of that to last her a lifetime.

After unloading the car, hanging her clothes, and loading the dresser drawers, she realized that she was hungry. She went to the kitchen to make some coffee and got a frozen bagel to heat in the microwave. As was said, Stacey had planned things to suit her and her alone. She sat on the chair and put her coffee beside her on the table and looked out the window in the great room. There was soft music playing because that is the first thing she had done. She had to have the sound of the music. The view from the window was spectacular. The woods surrounding her cabin were thick and filled with birds and small animals. She saw a doe and her fawn a distance from the cabin. There was a small pond some distance behind the cabin that the animals used as a watering hole so Stacey knew she would see wonderful things while she lived here. It was full dark by now and the rain that had threatened earlier was upon her. The sound of the rain in the trees and on the roof was like a symphony. The roof was covered with fir fronds and that softened any sound that came from the rain. Stacey sat in the chair by the wood stove and watched as the lightening in the distance lit up the sky. The cabin was warm from the stove and she was so at peace that she knew she had done the right thing. She still didn't know why but only that it was right.

As Stacey sat and night fell, she was remembering the beginning. It was so many years ago now that the need to do the things she had done began. She had no regrets even though perhaps she should. She had been a good wife and the death of her husband had not been at her hand. Fate had stepped in and taken him, as was his destiny. They had no family other than each other therefore no one would be left to mourn them. Her parents had died while she was in college and before she met her husband. That is where the money had come from. Her parents had been quite well-off and had died together in a car accident. She was an only child and all of the money had come to her. She had invested it wisely and for some unknown reason had never told her husband or anyone else that she had the money. When this need to leave came over her several years ago, she liquidated her portfolio and went totally to cash. The cash had been put into a lock box at the bank that was handling the bills that were drafted against her account. Several weeks ago, she had made a trip to the bank and had taken enough cash out of the lock box to last her for a very long time. If she ran low or needed anything, she had access to more. All that she owned - the cabin and land, and her little car - were in her new name. Nobody but the bank knew her name except her. Her name was Morgan.

SECTION 4

During the preparation for leaving, she had seen to it that the front of the cabin remained fairly untouched. That is as to appearance. She had strengthened the door and the two windows and had put pull down shades at the windows that remained down at all times. The front door had a double lock on it and it remained locked at all times. The old fashioned porch sagged here and there but other than making it safe, it looked the same. However, the back of the cabin was another story all together. She had new windows installed that were bigger and had lovely pull drapes to cover them. The same drapes were in the front, but they remained pulled while the back drapes remained open to the view. She had installed on the gate down the road an electronic eye so that were anyone to venture through, she would instantly hear the alarm that would tell her someone was on the way up.

Now that she was in her new home, she also knew that protection was totally up to her. Her father had been a sports enthusiast and had taught Morgan how to hunt and shoot. None of these skills were needed in the life she just left but they would be needed now. In the living area was a large gun safe. She had several long-range rifles in it along with bow and arrows and several handguns and knives. Morgan was extremely proficient with all of these weapons, as she had made it her responsibility to keep up her skills over the years. The woods around the cabin were so dense that anyone that tried to travel through would get hopelessly lost. Her Grandmother had taught her how to cook, can and preserve food and she already had a garden ready to plant for the season. She was going to have a lot to keep her busy but again, she had no choice. No choice at all.

It had been a long day. Actually, several long days and fatigue was beginning to catch up with her. She made sure everything was secure and that the fire in the wood stove was banked, ready for morning. Going into her bedroom, she decided to take a long soak and then go to bed. As she climbed into the bed, it felt somewhat strange because, even though it was more than big enough for her, it still seemed small compared to the king-sized bed she had slept in with her husband for so many years. But it was so comfortable that she propped several pillows behind her bed, turned the light on, and got one of her favorite books to read. Finding that she couldn't keep her eyes open, she laid the book down, turned off the light, and once again went immediately to sleep.

When she awoke the next morning, it occurred to her that she was sleeping well. Always through her life she had trouble sleeping. She had insomnia and spent any nights reading or pacing because she couldn't sleep. Now, for some reason, she fell instantly to sleep and slept through the night, feeling totally refreshed upon waking. She was famished and decided it was time for a big breakfast but she still hadn't gone into town for perishables so she had to make do with another bagel and coffee. Deciding it was time to make the first of many trips to town, she dressed in her jeans and denim shirt. The only difference was that she wore buckskin boots that came over her jeans almost to her knees and a buckskin jacket and a wide brimmed bat. This was not unusual attire as she was, after all in the West. She didn't wear her glasses either. She felt that it was safe to look the way she did and she welcomed the fact that she knew nobody was looking for her. Again, she didn't know how she knew this but she knew. Morgan made quite a picture dressed this way. She was a tall long-legged woman at 5 feet 8 inches tall and weighing just less than 150 pounds. She was strong and lithe and walked with an ease of knowing who she was. Her hair was just longer than shoulder length and was going gray. She wore it loose or braided depending on her mood.

Taking the little car out of the garage, she drove to the gate and got out. The ground was muddy but not too bad as she opened the gate and drove through. Closing the gate behind her, she turned her car towards town. The drive was long because the cabin was isolated and it took half of the morning just to get to town. She stopped at a camping store and bought two lanterns and a cooler large enough to fit into the trunk of her car. She also bought a sleeping bag and some ammunition. She was friendly but formal and gave an air of substance. No one would want to get close to this woman. She then went to a department store and bought some additional items to make her cabin more to her liking again with the same cool attitude. Colorful throws, more pillows and candles. Only then did she go to the grocery store.

Morgan bought fresh vegetables and fruit, some milk, eggs, and butter. She didn't need bread as she planned to bake her own but she did need meat until she could hunt. She bought enough to fill the cooler and added ice, packed the other groceries around the cooler and headed for home. She stopped on the way out of town and filled the car with gas so that if she needed to leave in a hurry that would not be a problem. When she left the town, all that could have been said about her was that she was new to the area, friendly enough but standoffish. By the time she drove, the sun rose early, as did Morgan. She ate a huge breakfast of bacon, eggs, toast and coffee. She took a cup of coffee outside and walked around while drinking her last cup of the morning. Trying to decide where to start, she noticed that the garden needed attention. She put aside her cup, put on her gloves, and began to pull weeds. After the garden was clear of weeds, she began to plant the seedlings that were in the shed. She planted pole beans, tomatoes, squash, potatoes, green beans and melon. She had wild blueberries on the land as well as apple trees and peach trees. There would be plenty of fruit for canning and preserving. She watered the garden and then started hammering tall metal poles around the perimeter. With the poles in place, she strung chicken wire tight between the poles. This she knew would keep the deer out the garden. She was going to feed them cracked corn down by the pond anyway so hopefully they wouldn't want to raid her garden. She purposely didn't plant corn because she didn't want to have to fight the deer and the birds.

Her back ached and she was sore all over. She had always been active by playing tennis, jogging and going to the gym but this was using a whole other set of muscles and she was tired and sore. Deciding to call it a day, she went into the cabin and got cleaned up. She wanted to be outside so she took a lounge chair from the shed and put it by the back door. She could sit there with her feet up on the back step, tip back and watch her world go by. Sipping iced tea and sitting quietly for several minutes brought the animals out. Over by the pond, the doe and her fawn emerged. She picked a handful of wild flowers as she walked and put them into a small vase when she entered the back door of the utility room. The vase would look nice on the table and she intended to get more plants for the cabin but for now these would do just fine.

Darkness had begun to fall and she prepared for bed. Sitting on the couch with pillows all around and looking at the fire in the wood stove she began to think about her old home. Had she had a television or a radio, she would have known that a piece of her husband's boat had been found among other wreckage that could identify that it was indeed his boat. He was presumed dead and a memorial service was held for both husband and wife. Her old house had been sold with the furniture in it to a couple with two small children. The money that was raised from the sale of their estate went to charity as their wills had instructed, as they had no family to leave anything of value to. Morgan was very proud to be of American-Indian heritage and her half of the estate went to the Cherokee Nation for help in building schools. Her husband's half of the estate went to his favorite charities and so it was done. She put those thoughts away not to be brought out again. Concentrating on her new life would take all of her skill and energy. Going from a modern home with all of the things that the modern and electronic world has to a more basic existence would tax her strength and courage, but she knew that it was right. She was more comfortable in her skin than ever before. She was finally going to live her life the way it was meant to be lived.

SECTION 5

Another busy day, and she was off to bed and immediately to sleep. It was the middle of the afternoon, and she was about to return to what she was starting to call home. Unpacking the car and putting everything away took the rest of the afternoon and then she began to cook. She made herself a beautiful steak with a large tossed green salad and fresh tomatoes. A baked potato covered with butter and sour cream topped off the meal, and she sat at her little gate-leg table and enjoyed her first real meal since leaving her old home. After cleaning up from her meal, she decided to take a walk around the place and work off some of the food. Stepping out the back door she startled two squirrels that were playing in an oak tree near the cabin. She laughed out loud at their antics, and the noise that her laugh made startled them. It was going to take some getting used to; all of this quiet but she looked forward to the quiet. Noise pollution had always been one of her pet peeves. It disturbed her because she couldn't hear the land talking to her with all of the city noise. Here she could hear the land.

Morgan began her walk around the backside of her property. She was amazed to see so many plants and flowers. There were ferns growing wild among the trees and wild flowers everywhere she looked. Over by the back corner of the cabin near the window in her bedroom was a large tangle of wild roses. Her first thought was to thin and prune and she would have such a lovely scent coming into her bedroom in the night. There were birds that she could not identify and she made a mental note to get a book so that she would know them all. The grass was just wild and she planned on keeping it that way. She didn't want the place to look like it was being regularly maintained. She would keep the area around the back of the house trimmed but not so much that it still didn't look well from the woods. Over in the trees, the squirrels chattered and the birds sang. Morgan was content and felt no reason for alarm.

Suddenly the alarm for the gate went off. She slammed the chair to the ground, ran into the cabin, and grabbed her shotgun. Going to the door and looking out the window, she couldn't see around the bend to the gate but the alarm didn't lie. Someone was trying to get on to her property. She waited silently and still she saw nothing. Running to the back of the house, she went quietly out the door and around to the corner of the cabin that was covered by shrubs. Standing quietly, she listened and hear voices. Men's voices that were angry. She moved slowly towards the shrubs on the other side of the drive. It was twilight and she was dressed all in blue so that she was almost invisible in the open. She was able to get close enough to hear the two men and what they were saying. They sounded drunk and as if they were looking for a fight. They had not been able to get through the gate because the lock had held. It appeared that the fight was about whether or not to break the lock. They were only looking for a place to sleep off their drunk because they couldn't go home in the condition they were in, but to break the lock took more energy than either man had. They compromised by getting into their truck and driving away to the next town and trying to find a place to lay low until they could sober up.

Morgan stayed still for some time after they drove off, making sure that they didn't come back. She walked down to the gate, staying inside the tree line, and inspected the lock. It had not been damaged, so she turned and, still in the tree line, walked back to the cabin. It was full dark now so she put the chair that had been left outside in the shed and went in through the back door. She left the shotgun by the door and went on into the kitchen for a cup of coffee. Her excursion down to the gate had made her hot and sweaty so she took another quick bath and prepared for bed. She banked the fire in the wood stove even though it wasn't really cold. She knew that in the morning the stove and the warmth it provided would be needed. She slept with her window open just a crack so that she could breathe the fresh air and hear the night sounds. Climbing into bed with a good book and soft music, she was content and again asleep before her head had barely hit the pillow.

SECTION 6

The next morning, Morgan was woken by the sound of thunder and rain. It was a soft rain and she was grateful that she wouldn't have to water the garden today but it also meant that she would have to stay indoors or work in the shed. She ate a good breakfast and, wearing her usual jeans and denim shirt, went to the shed. She wasn't wearing boots but buckskin moccasins. The shed was a mess because of all the moving and hauling and she took the opportunity of the wet day to organize the shed. Putting all of the gardening supplies in one corner, she set up a potting bench in front of the window and put all of her potting supplies under the bench. She had starts of Boston fern, Wandering Jew, and Aloe Vera plants. She also had some English Ivy. She wanted the ivy for the side of the shed to soften the look, but the others she would take into the cabin. She started potting her plants and humming while she worked. She stopped because she didn't know what she was humming. It wasn't anything familiar to her and it was just a constant hum with an off and on beat.

After she potted all of the plants and had taken them into the cabin, she went back to the shed and began to clean all of the tools. She had been taught at a very young age that when you use a tool, you clean it before you put it away. She had a pegboard that she had mounted over a small workbench and she hung each tool in its place. Morgan was not a stickler for neatness but she did like order. In a large house, there was more room to spread out all of the day's things, but in the cabin, space was at a premium, and in order to function without frustration, she needed it neat. She had grabbed an apple and eaten it for lunch, and was still at work in the shed when it came time to call it a day. Looking around she was pleased with her progress. The tools were clean and in their place. Her potting bench was set up efficiently. The floor was swept and the other things she needed for the place were near at hand, but there was still plenty of room to move about. She locked the shed and headed into the cabin for the night.

After a dinner of new potatoes and fresh green beans and a salad, Morgan readied herself for bed. She sat on the couch and put wood on the fire. It wasn't cold but there was a chill and the cabin warmed up quickly. Sipping a cup of hot tea, she let her mind take her where it would. She thought of her husband. There's had been a good marriage. They were so much in love when they married. They had Church on Sunday and a small group of friends but none that Morgan would ever bare her soul to. She and her husband talked but didn't really have much time together as one or the other was coming or going at all hours. He was in love with his boat and she didn't resent this at all as long as he accepted the fact that she didn't want to be on the water. It worked out fine because while he was on the boat she was doing her own thing with her friends. Morgan had time to read and listen to music but there was always something missing and she couldn't put her finger on it. It was a call or a pull in a direction that she didn't know. It was only during the past few years that she knew that she had to leave. There was something she had to do and it had to be done alone. Therefore, she began her preparations. She followed her instinct in making the preparations because she didn't know why this was happening to her. Her husband noticed nothing different because he was caught up in his world of business, travel, and the boat. Her thoughts and memories of him were happy, and when she thought of him, it was with warmth and love. She was relieved that he didn't suffer during his death. Again, she didn't know how she knew this, she just did.

The rain had continued all day and was still a very slow misty rain. She banked the fire for the night and headed for the bedroom after locking up. Crawling into bed, she didn't even turn on the light or pick up a book because she knew she would sleep immediately and she did.

SECTION 7

Morgan was up early the next morning and had eaten breakfast, straightened the cabin, and stoked the fires. She had seen to Horse before the carpenter arrived. He did as she warned and honked the horn before getting out of his truck. He had another man with him that he had told Morgan about, and they both stayed in the truck until Morgan went out with Wolf. She leaned down and talked to Wolf while holding her arms around his neck. She motioned for the carpenter to slowly get out of the truck and come towards them. As the man opened the door and climbed down, Morgan straightened, and with one hand on Wolf, she walked towards the carpenter. When she reached him, she introduced him to Wolf and told him to put out his hand so that Wolf could smell his scent. The carpenter wasn't afraid at all for some reason and put his hand out and held in still for Wolf. After a moment, Wolf took a step forward and sniffed the man's hand and then began to lick him and bounce around. Well, thought Morgan that was easy enough. The process was duplicated with the helper and all was well. If Wolf accepted a man then Morgan knew that she had nothing to fear.

The carpenter had brought the new windows and door and all of the lumber in his truck so he got right to work. He tore out the old windows and immediately installed the newer bigger double paned windows and trimmed them out. While Morgan puttered in the cabin, he removed the front door and replaced it with the new front door that had a heavy dead lock bolt on it. He trimmed out the inside of the door and window and went outside to start on the porch. After he left the front room, Morgan came and painted the new trim around the door and window. It didn't take long and it looked so bright and cheerful. The paint dried quickly, so by the time the furniture delivery arrived, the room was ready for the furniture. The deliverymen didn't have to deal with Wolf because he had left for his daily inspection of his territory knowing that Morgan was in safe hands. Bringing the furniture inside didn't take long and the truck barreled down the drive headed back to town.

Now the fun began for Morgan. She pulled the queen sized bed out and made it up with the softest of sheets and quilts. She folded it back in place and put it on the far wall with two chairs on each side and end tables between the chairs and the couch. The wood stove was on the other wall and the carpenter had already attached the flu pipe, cutting a hole in the ceiling, and took it through the roof. He trimmed out the hole and Morgan painted the trim when he was finished. She put the recliner over by the other window facing into the room but also giving a great view of the front of the property. You still couldn't see the gate from here but that was exactly how she wanted it. She took the old pull down shades away and hung the sheer curtains behind the draw drapes. While the carpenters worked outside, Morgan worked inside. She set candles and the pottery bowl on the coffee table. She hung the paintings she had bought and brought in the throw pillows and scatter rugs. She stood back to look at her handiwork and was pleased. She had the game table set up under the other window knowing that it was easily moved to wherever they wanted to sit and play. She could imagine the cold winter nights when she, Willa, and Mr. Stone would sit and play cards with the wood stove keeping them all warm.

The carpenters knocked and told her that they were finished for the day and would return the next morning. She thanked them, and as they drove away, she looked around at the day's progress and was pleased. They had trimmed out the new windows and door. They had leveled the front porch and railing and put new steps going down to the walkway. They had also put in a ramp with a very gradual grade for Willa's chair. She had made sure that the front door was wide enough for Willa and her chair to pass through. Tomorrow they would start to take the porch around the corner to the side of the house. The walkway was river rock and they were going to bring brick to make a side walk that could accommodate Willa and her chair.

Morgan went inside and lit a fire in the new stove with wood from a pretty basket sitting next to the stove. It lit easily and drew perfectly so there was no smoke in the house, only warmth. She made herself a light supper and went out to care for Horse. She spent quite a while in the ham with him as she felt that she had been neglecting him lately but he seemed completely content because Mr. Stone came so often. Morgan had told Mr. Stone not to come for a few days because she wanted to surprise Willa and him with the new renovations at the same time.

When she left the barn and left the shed for the cabin, Wolf was standing there waiting on her. Together they went into the cabin and having already eaten herself, she put a bowl of stew down for Wolf. While he ate, Morgan bathed and put on her nightdress and came to the kitchen to get a cup of tea and clean Wolf's bowl. She stoked the fire and sat on the couch and read for a while until her eyes began to droop. She got up and banked the fire in the new living room and the great room and went into the bedroom with Wolf on her heels. Laying down, she pulled up the covers and was asleep before she knew it.

The next day dawned sunny and cold and the process of the carpenter's arrival was repeated with Wolf. It didn't take as long this time because Wolf had accepted the two men and they could get right to work. Morgan noticed that they had the two swings on the trailer and when she asked the carpenter, he told her that the work was going much faster than he anticipated and he thought he would be able to hand the swings today. She left them to their work and went back through the house out to the barn. She let Horse out into the corral so he could enjoy the sunshine and walked down to the pond to see if the doe and fawn had left tracks that morning. They had indeed been there early and she was pleased that they still came daily to drink. Going back to the house, she was impatient for the men to finish the work, as she couldn't wait to show Willa and Mr. Stone.

She decided to bake so that she wouldn't get in their way and whipped up a batch of brownies filled with fresh shelled pecans. Then she made a coconut four layer cake with butter cream icing. She had invited the Stone's for supper the next night and she put a beef brisket on to marinate all night. She took some of the brownies out to the carpenters and they were grateful for the break in the day. They had actually finished the porch and were in the process of hanging the swings. They had used pine for the porch so that it wouldn't have to be painted. She wanted the outside wood to look as natural as possible. All that was left to do was the short brick walk from the drive to the ramp and they said they would finish that tomorrow. So instead of five days, it was only going to take three and Morgan was thrilled.

After the men left for the day, she walked down to the gate making sure it was locked and then walked to the barn. She whistled and Horse came in from the corral directly into his stall. Morgan gave him fresh water and oats and plenty of fresh hay and talked to him for a while telling him all about the plans for the cabin. Leaving him for the night and locking the door behind her, she went through the shed and looked down but Wolf wasn't there. It gave her a start but she decided that he was just late in coming home and would be back soon. She went into the cabin and fixed herself some soup with fresh bread and then went to take her bath and get ready for the night. Coming out of the bedroom, she looked out and Wolf was nowhere to be found. Trying not to panic, Morgan sat on the couch and tried to read but couldn't concentrate because of the absence of Wolf. She went on to bed but kept getting up in the night looking out the door for signs of Wolf and he never appeared.

The next morning, the carpenters were early and laid the sidewalk with bricks, filling in any cracks with sand. They brushed the sand back and forth until it had dropped down through the cracks in the brick, and she knew that until spring it would have to do. She planned on putting in a better walkway for Willa come spring but couldn't do it now because the snows were coming soon. Thanking the carpenters for all their fine work, she paid them in cash and watched as they drove away. She was very pleased with the way the front of the house looked but was filled with anxiety about Wolf.

Mr. Stone and Willa were coming early so they could eat and get back home before it got too late. Morgan went in and the aroma of the brisket made her stomach growl. She had added new potatoes, baby carrots, and boiler onions to the brisket. She had fresh green beans and a salad with homemade bread. The desert was to be the coconut cake she baked yesterday. She set the gate-leg table with pretty place mats and dishes and went to freshen up before they arrived. Wolf still hadn't shown up and she was getting more and more fretful.

Hearing the Stones car pull come up the drive, she hurried to the front porch to meet them. When they stopped the car at the sidewalk, both of them had dropped their jaws in surprise. Morgan jumped up and down as Mr. Stone got out of the car and walked around to help Willa out with her chair. As he pushed her chair up the brick walk and onto the ramp to the porch, they were both speechless with surprise. How did you do it so fast, they asked? Morgan just laughed and held the front door open. Mr. Stone pushed Willa's chair through the door and again, he just stopped and looked with awe. They were both totally surprised at what had been accomplished in such a short time. Morgan went around showing them all of the new things, and then when she got to the sofa and showed them that it had a queen-sized bed in it, Willa began to cry. Morgan ran to her and kneeled down and put her arms around the sweet woman. Willa just couldn't' believe that Morgan had done all of this for them and Morgan assured her that yes it was for them but it was for herself as well. She needed to open the whole cabin up and enjoy it for what it was, her home. After much oooing and ahhhing, they went in to supper. Mr. Stone could tell that something was wrong but hesitated to bring it up and spoil such a delicious meal, however when they were finished with the suburb food and groaning from being so full, he asked Morgan what was wrong. That is when she told them about Wolf.

Mr. Stone immediately got up and put on his heavy coat and said he would be back. He went out the back door and Willa visited with Morgan while she cleared the table and put the kitchen to rights. They were sitting at the table drinking tea when Mr. Stone returned. He motioned for Morgan to come to the door and in doing so he frowned over her head at his wife and shook his head. When Morgan got to the door, she saw Wolf wrapped in Mr. Stone's coat laying on the step to the cabin.

SECTION 8

Morgan was dumb struck as she looked down at Wolf. Mr. Stone assured her that he was alive but they needed to get him inside out of the cold. Lifting him gently, Mr. Stone brought Wolf in by the fire and laid him in his blanket by the stove. Willa had instantly gone to the kitchen to boil water knowing that whatever was wrong they would need it. Mr. Stone carefully took his coat from around Wolf and there were several gashes on his side. He had a few smaller gashes on his muzzle but the side injuries looked to be the most serious. Mr. Stone told Morgan as he tried to move the hair away so that he could get a better look at the injuries that he found Wolf down by the pond. He was just sitting on his haunches but didn't seem to have the energy to continue to the cabin. He had lost a lot of blood and had traveled a long way to get as far as he had. Morgan sat on the floor holding his head in her lap and patting him gently. Willa carefully rolled over with the hot water but Mr. Stone said that he was going to have to shave the hair away before he could clean the wounds and stitch them up. Morgan looked up at him with questions in her eyes and he reassured her that he used to run cattle when he was young and knew how to do this. Wolf had lost so much blood that he was in shock and wouldn't feel the pain as he was going to swab the area with a solution that would deaden it for the most part.

He quickly went into the bathroom and got Morgan's razor and returned to the fire. He headed for the barn running as he went and came back with a bottle of a clear liquid. Morgan didn't even know that it was there, and he said that he had brought it out while he had been looking after Horse while she was sick, just in case of an emergency like this. He got a needle and some fishing line and boiled them in some water on the stove. He gave the needle and the line to Willa and told her to thread the line through the eye of the needle but not to tie any knots in it. He got sharp scissors from the kitchen and boiled them too. All the while Morgan murmured to Wolf and he lay still in her lap. Finally, Mr. Stone was ready and he swabbed the area where the deepest cuts were. Wolf didn't even whimper and he began to carefully shave away the hair so that he could see the cuts better.

When he was ready, he cleaned the wounds thoroughly and reached for the needle that Willa held out to him. Carefully, he pulled the skin together and put in a stitch and tied it off with a knot. He told Morgan that Wolf was lucky because the cuts didn't go into the muscle and were only in the outer layer of skin. Slowly, he would put in a stitch and tie it off, again and again until all of the wounds were closed. He cleaned the scratches on Wolfs face and rose to go to the bathroom once again. He came back with one of Morgan's older sheets and tore it into long strips. Taking one strip, he wrapped it securely around Wolf and tied it off so that the wound would be covered. He told Morgan that this would have to be done daily until the wounds healed and he could remove the stitches. Willa had gone to the kitchen and returned with a warm bowl of stew and some fresh water and Morgan put these by Wolf's head. He lifted his head enough to drink a bit but didn't seem interested in the stew. Mr. Stone said that the most important thing was to keep him still and warm and get him to drink as much as possible.

While he took all of the clutter away and put it up or disposed of it, Morgan continued to hold Wolf in her lap and slowly rock back and forth as you would a baby. Wolf reached again for some water and then laid his head on his blanket and closed his eyes. Mr. Stone checked him and said that he was sleeping and that was the best thing for him. All three of them left him by the fire and went back to the table where Willa had made tea for them. Morgan was silent. She didn't know what to think and then she asked Mr. Stone if he could tell what had happened. Mr. Stone hesitated because he knew that the answer to her question was going to put her in danger but he would not lie to Morgan. He told her that it was most certainly a cat that had gotten Wolf and that he was very lucky to have gotten away with his life. Morgan just sat for a moment and then a look of pure determination came over her face. She got up from the table and went over to check on Wolf, then told the Stone's that at first light she would take Horse and they would go and find the cat. No more had to be said as they all knew that she meant to kill it.

She asked if they could stay at the cabin for the next two days as it was the weekend and she hoped to be able to get the cat before the weekend was over. Mr. Stone and Willa were anxious to stay as he had closed the store for the weekend and Wolf would need tending. Morgan told them that she was going to pack and that she would not be back until the cat was dead. Under normal circumstances, Morgan's eyes were a bright green but when she was angry they turned a deep emerald and that is what they were now. The Stone's knew better than to argue or try to talk her out of going, so they just reassured her that while she was gone they would see to Wolf. Mr. Stone told her that if she weren't back by Sunday night, he would call an old retired employee of his and have him open the store. They did insist that she take the two-way radio in case she got hurt, they could get help for her.

Morgan went into the bedroom and began to throw some extra socks in her saddlebag. She also threw in extra gloves and some thermal underwear. Going into the kitchen, she saw that Willa had put together several meals that she could eat out on the trail and at a campsite. Morgan went to the shed and got the sleeping bag down. She also got a burlap bag and filled it with oats for horse. All of these things she left by the door in the shed. She got two rifles down and cleaned them both. She put extra ammunition in her pack and went to sit with Wolf. The three adults sat quietly and talked until it was time for bed. Morgan went into the front room and pulled the bed out and made it comfortable for Mr. Stone and Willa. She added wood to the stove and told them good night. She went to her room and sat on the bed but couldn't even think of lying down. Getting up, she went into Wolf and sat by him leaning up against the wall and stroking his head and neck while he slept. She fell asleep next to Wolf and that is where she woke the next morning.

She quietly got a thermos of coffee and left the house without making any noise, as it was still dark outside. She went to the barn and threw a saddle on Horse and tied the bedroll and pack onto the saddle along with the bag of oats. She put one rifle in the saddle scabbard and carried the other in her arms. She was dressed warmly with her thermal underwear and jeans and flannel shirt. She had her buckskin poncho on and gloves and also covered her face and ears to protect herself from the cold. She opened the barn door, and mounting Horse led him out into the yard and around the cabin towards the high country. She didn't look back because she knew that she would come back with the cat or not at all. She had written a will the night before stating that if anything happened to her, Mr. Stone and Willa were her heirs and were to receive her entire estate. Morgan was fully aware that she was putting herself and Horse in danger, but it had to be done.

They rode for a long distance before reaching the trail up into the mountains. Morgan dismounted and let Horse rest for a bit before they began the climb up. It would not be an easy journey but she knew that Horse was as ready as she was to avenge Wolf. Mounting once again, they began to climb. Morgan let Horse go at his own pace and his own trail while she kept her eyes on the rocks and undergrowth around her. They stopped again around noon and took a break. Morgan found fresh water for Horse, and he drank his fill while she ate a sandwich and drank a cup of coffee. She didn't tarry once they had eaten, but pushed on upwards. She knew the cat was up there and she intended to kill him.

As night began to fall, Morgan stopped at a clearing and set up a fire pit. She knew she was close to fresh water and that was the main thing that they would need. She let Horse drink and feed him his oats and then staked him close to her under the trees. Morgan drank some coffee and ate some stew that she warmed up over the campfire. She threw her sleeping bag down near the fire, and with her rifle at hand, tried to get a little rest. It was quiet and the moon was full so she had plenty of light. Horse couldn't rest either as he stomped around and snorted. Finally, after catching a nap, the dawn began to come and Morgan packed up the camp and mounted Horse and continued to travel up the mountain. They were nearing a bend when instinct made Morgan look up. On top of the rocks, at the bend in the trail, stood the cat. It was a large mountain lion and the look of hate was all over him. Morgan didn't even have time to raise her rifle and aim before he had jumped and knocked her off of the saddle onto the ground. Horse was rearing and bucking trying to get the cat off of him but the cat held on and was trying to bite Horse on the neck. Morgan had taken a hard fall but not so hard that she let go of her rifle. The noise was incredible. Horse was bucking and rearing and snorting and blowing and the cat was growling and screaming and trying to hold on to Horse. The only thing that saved Horse at all was the fact that Morgan had put the saddle on him because the cat had his claws firmly embedded in the saddle and not the Horse. He was trying desperately to bite Horse on the neck when Morgan took aim with her Remington and shot him. He fell from Horse but wasn't dead, though mortally injured.

Morgan was able to get off a second shot within seconds and the cat lay still. She regained her feet and walked over to where the cat lay in the dirt and saw that he was indeed dead. She grabbed Horse's reins and began to try to settle him down. It took quite a while to get him to settle but she walked him over away from the cat and gave him water to drink using her poncho as a bowl. She tied him to a tree a distance from the cat, got her knife out, and walked back over to the cat and skinned him. She threw his carcass over the side of the trail for the scavengers. She wrapped the pelt in a burlap bag, picked up her rifle, and went to get Horse. When she mounted him and headed back down the mountain, Horse went at a steady pace sensing that the danger was over and he could take his time getting back to the cabin. They rode late rather than camp out again and it was well past dark when they arrived home.

Mr. Stone and Willa heard them in the barn and Mr. Stone went out to see what he could do to help. Morgan had no idea how she looked. Her hair had come out of its braid, her head covering was lost, and her poncho was filthy and covered with blood. Horse didn't look much better but at least he wasn't cut. Mr. Stone said that he would take care of Horse and she should go inside and take care of herself. She pointed to the burlap bag, and Mr. Stone nodded and told her that he would stake it and help her get it ready for tanning in the morning. Morgan was so tired she could barely walk but she did walk and met Willa by the back door. Even better than that, she met Wolf by the back door too. She kneeled down and took his face in her hands and he looked at her with eyes that told her he knew that she had avenged him. She told him that he need not be afraid of that cat again, and he seemed to smile before slowly turning and walking back to his blanket by the stove and gingerly laying down. Willa told her that he was recovering very quickly and had been up and walking around several time that day. The wounds were healing well and Mr. Stone thought the stitches could come out in another day or so.

Sensing Morgan's exhaustion, Willa hurried her into the bedroom and told her to take her bath, and when she was done, Willa would have something ready for her to eat. Morgan didn't realize how hungry she was until Willa mentioned food, but she had to get clean before she could eat. She tossed her clothes on the floor and climbed into the tub, scrubbing herself and washing the dirt, dust, and blood out of her hair. She dried off and put on her nightdress, a robe, and slippers. When she came out of her bedroom, Willa had set the table with cold fried chicken, potato salad, baked beans, and biscuits with gravy. Morgan ate until she could eat no more and after thanking Willa for the wonderful meal, she started to go to the barn to check on Horse. Before she could even get to the door, Mr. Stone came in and said that all was well, he had washed Horse down and dried him off. He brushed and curried him all the while talking to him. After plenty of fresh hay and oats, Horse was settled for the night. Mr. Stone told Willa and Morgan that he had staked the cat's pelt out and it looked to be about 5 feet long and he estimated that he was probably around 125 pounds. Morgan looked at Mr. Stone and saw in his eyes how lucky she had been but she knew that luck had nothing to do with it. Her ancestors and her Lord kept her safe and gave her the courage to go after and kill the mountain lion before he could kill again.

She again thanked the Stone's for all of their help, and they all once again went to bed, but this time Morgan took Wolf with her, and he slept on his blanket by the stove in her room. Upon waking the next morning, Mr. Stone examined Wolf and said that another day or so and he should be fine. He and Willa were going back to town but he would come back and take the stitches out in two days. Morgan looked deeply into their eyes and said thank you. They hugged her and went out to the car. Morgan watched them out of sight around the curve in the drive and, turning, went back into the cabin. She went out to take care of Horse, and although he seemed a bit tired, there wasn't a mark on him. She left him in the barn and went into the house only to find Wolf standing up waiting on his breakfast. She fed him and he went over by the stove and lay down and went back to sleep. Morgan tided up the cabin and took a cup of tea over to the couch where she sat and watched Wolf sleep. How blessed she was to have her wonderful Wolf by her side once again; to have Horse in the ham safe and sound and to have the Stone's well and on their way home. Yes, she was truly blessed, and she gave thanks once again to her ancestors and her Lord.

SECTION 9

Mr. Stone was as good as his word and returned in two days to remove Wolf's stitches. In the meantime, Morgan had taken special care of Horse and he seemed to be fully recovered. Wolf was still weak but was feeling much better if his appetite was any indication of his health. Mr. Stone said that the stitches were ready to come out, and Wolf lay in Morgan's lap while he removed them. Wolf didn't move, nor did he let out a whimper, and Morgan whispered to him while Mr. Stone removed the stitches. Once it was all over, Wolf stood and shook himself out and headed for the door. He looked back over his shoulder at Morgan and she looked at Mr. Stone. He nodded to her, and she rose and went over, opening the door to let Wolf out. He went out and walked towards the pond a few steps slower than normal but seemingly his old self once again. Mr. Stone told Morgan to let him do what he wanted, as he knew best about himself. They stood together and watched Wolf as he looked around and walked away. It was as if he was scanning his territory to make sure that nobody had messed with his stuff while he was sick. Morgan and Mr. Stone laughed together and turned going back into the cabin. She asked him to stay for tea but he said that he needed to get back as there was a fierce storm coming in. Morgan had not listened to the weather yet so she turned it on and heard the warning of the storm to come. She hurried Mr. Stone on his way assuring him that she and Horse and Wolf would be fine. They had plenty of wood and food for him to go and be with Willa. She watched as he drove away and putting on her poncho that she had cleaned thoroughly after the fight with the cat, walked down to the gate to double lock it, and make sure it was secure. The wind was picking up and she hurried back to the barn. Going in, she brought plenty of hay down for Horse and made sure he had food and water. Closing and locking the barn, she went to the cabin and looked for Wolf. He was still at the pond so she let him stay as long as she could see him. She went into the cabin and tilled all of the bins and basket with wood for the stoves. She lit the little heater in the bathroom and checked the cupboard to see if she needed to make a trip to the root cellar.

Hearing a crash outside the utility room door, Morgan grabbed her rifle and ran to the door throwing it open with the rifle at the ready. Laughing at herself, she lowered the rifle and picked up the lawn chair that had blown into the side of the cabin. She brought it inside and left it in the utility room. Looking up, she saw Wolf headed back towards the cabin and she went out on the step, closing the door so as not to let the heat out, to wait for him. Once he was close to her, she opened the door and he went in and directly to his blanket where he laid down and went to sleep. He was still weak but she knew that he was going to be just fine. The wind grew stronger as the day passed and Morgan moved from room to room looking out the windows at the approaching storm. It started to snow, lightly at first and then so heavily that she couldn't see the road anymore. She was so thankful that she was secure and warm but worried about Mr. Stone. She keyed the radio, and when Willa answered, she asked if he had made it back safely. Willa assured her that he had indeed made it home and that they were in for the duration of the storm. Morgan assured Willa of the same and they keyed off of the radio. It had gotten dark and the snow was falling so fast and so heavily that Morgan was glad she had given Horse extra food and water knowing that she wouldn't have to go to the barn again for a while.

The wind blew like nothing Morgan had ever seen. It appeared to be snowing sideways and it was snowing hard. She kept walking around and looking out. Every time she did, she could see less and less and the snow was beginning to really accumulate. There was nothing to do, but wait it out so she made some tea and got the lanterns down knowing that she would probably lose power. Hopefully it would continue to snow and not rain. Ice over snow was not good. She sat on the couch and sipped her tea and decided she would try to make one trip to the barn before nightfall. She pulled on her boots and her poncho, covered her head and with a flashlight opened the back door. The wind almost knocked her down it was so strong. She went holding on to the rope hand over hand and made it to the shed. Opening the door and getting inside was such a relief that when she went into the barn and saw Horse just standing there pleasantly, she thought she had just wasted a trip. She took advantage of anyway and filled the water trough and got down even more hay for him. He had plenty of oats so she patted him and talked to him for just a minute and then headed back to the cabin. Again, when she opened the shed door to the breezeway, the wind almost knocked her down. Thankful that she had the rope to guide her, she again went hand over back towards the cabin, but when she got halfway there, she felt the rope come loose, and she was holding a rope that wasn't attached to anything anymore. The guide rope had come loose at both ends. Morgan dropped to her knees knowing that to move would be a disaster until she could figure out where she was.

She couldn't see any light and the only thing she could hear was the howling of the wind. She was very cold despite her animal hide coverings but concentrated with all her being and calmness came over her. She stayed on her knees and slowly began to move. She didn't have any idea what direction she was going in but something was making her move. Inch by inch she moved, almost crawling on her hands and knees. It seemed like hours but Morgan wasn't afraid. She was in God's hands and would go in the direction he led.

Suddenly, she heard a noise right in front of her. Listening hard, she began to laugh out loud. It was the howl of a wolf that she had heard. Morgan stood up and took one step reaching out her hand and touching the door to her cabin. She opened the door and Wolf was jumping all over her licking her face with joy.

Morgan got out of her wet things and into a warm bath. Putting on her nightdress and warm robe and slippers she went to the kitchen and made tea. The minute she lifted the mug to take a sip, the lights went out. She had only been back inside for about half an hour. How fortunate to have had hot water for a bath and to get settled before losing her power. There was a lantern at her fingertips that she lit and holding her tea, leaving the lantern in the bar, she settled on the couch. There was a need for the generator as it was late and Morgan was ready for bed. She knew everything would be fine in the freezer as long as the door remained closed. If the power were still off come morning, she might have to start the generator but she would worry about that come morning. Sitting on the couch after stoking all of the stoves, Morgan gave thanks to her ancestors and her Lord. After finishing her tea, she motioned to Wolf and they went to bed to sleep through a dreamless night.

Sometime, during the night, the snow changed to a fine mist that froze completely covering the snow with ice. When Morgan rose and looked out, she thought she was looking at twinkling stars in the yard. The dawn was pink and the mist had stopped, making her yard look like a pink fairy wonderland that glistened. She let Wolf out and giggled as he slipped and slid on the frozen ground. He didn't stay out long and when he came back in, she fed him some canned food and filled his water bowl. She dressed warmly so that she could go out to the shed and turn on the generator. Morgan needed coffee. She no sooner touched the door when the power came back on. What a relief not to have to start up that nerve-wracking generator. Pulling off her poncho and changing from boots to moccasins, she went back to the kitchen and made coffee and a big breakfast of ham and eggs and toast. After eating and clearing the kitchen, she poured herself another cup of coffee and went to the couch to call Willa. She keyed the radio and Willa answered immediately. They both had been worried about the other and were relieved to find that all was well. Morgan didn't tell Willa about going outside last night and getting lost. Some things were better left unsaid.

The snow melted quickly as the temperatures rose and within a day or so, Morgan could drive to town since she had the big truck and four-wheel drive. She told Willa she was coming in because she needed more rope. She didn't tell her why. After seeing to Horse, and letting a fully recovered Wolf out, she left her cabin and headed to town. Arriving in town, she immediately went to the hardware store where Mr. Stone and Willa were so happy to see her. She sat for a long time with Willa talking about the storm and the lack of power. Willa had made apple turnovers that melted in your mouth and they drank hot tea and visited. Mr. Stone was out in the store talking to customers as he normally was. When she felt like she had stayed long enough, she told Willa goodbye and got her rope telling Mr. Stone goodbye and left.

She stopped at the grocery store to stock up on milk, butter and eggs and headed on back to the cabin. It had been good to get out but she was already anxious to get home. She didn't like to stay away for long. On arriving back home, it was already late afternoon. Morgan unloaded the truck and put it up. She went to Horse and spent some time with him telling him that tomorrow they would go ride if the weather held. Leaving him for the night, she headed for the cabin and Wolf was waiting on her. Everything was back to normal and normal was good. She and Wolf went inside and she locked the door behind her. She made them their supper, and after eating and setting the kitchen to rights, she added wood to the stove and sat down on the couch. Wolf was snoozing in his bed of blankets and Morgan had such a sense of well-being. She thanked her ancestors and her Lord and got up and went to bed.

The next morning dawned beautiful. There was still snow but only in patches and in the higher mountains. After a big breakfast, Morgan banked the stoves and letting Wolf out went to the barn and saddled Horse. She wasn't riding barebacked in the winter. She had her deerskin poncho and boots and her rifle. She mounted and they walked out of the barn into the beautiful morning. Horse was feeling his oats as he had been cooped up for quite some time and Morgan let him run. It felt so wonderful to be free and to be able to just run. After a while, he began to slow and walk at a steady pace. They visited the meadow where soon there would be wild flowers. They visited the creek that was running fast from all of the snowmelt off. They visited the outcrop of rock and just kept on riding. She stopped for lunch and gave Horse some water and an apple and ate an apple herself. Resting for a bit and enjoying the beauty around her, she once again gave thanks for all of her good fortune. She and Horse meandered around the land until it was time to head back to the cabin. They took their time and once returning home, she unsaddled Horse and brushed him good. Giving him fresh hay and water, she patted him as she left to go to the house.

Leaving the door to the shed, she saw Wolf waiting for her and together they went into the cabin. It wasn't full dark but it was cold and she really didn't want to stay out past dark right now. Before she could take off her outer clothing, the alarm went off to the gate. Morgan grabbed her rifle and for some reason stuck her 44-caliber handgun in the back of her belt under her poncho. She and Wolf went out the back door quietly and around the side of the house where they could see the drive. It was almost dark and Morgan motioned to Wolf to stand still and not to move. They watched as a man walked up the road. He had indeed climbed over the gate and for whatever reason was headed to the cabin. Morgan noted that he carried a rifle and was looking around the place as he walked. When he got within hearing distance, while remaining in the shadows and keeping her rifle aimed right at his heart, she told him in a commanding voice to stop. He just kept on coming and Wolf began to growl. Again Morgan told the man to stop, that he was trespassing on private property. He laughed at her and kept on coming. When he got within about forty feet from her she took one-step out into the light with her rifle aimed at his heart and told him again to stop. Wolf stepped out with her and bared his fangs and growled deep in his throat. Wolf had grown to be an imposing creature. He was as big as any wolf this guy had ever seen and he could tell that he would kill for this woman by the look in his eye. Morgan told him to put his rifle on the ground and kick it towards her. The man, keeping his eye on Wolf did as he was told. Morgan told him to turn around and start walking back the way he had come and not to come to her property again. The man said that he was only looking for a warm place to stay for the night. Morgan thought this was a pretty lame statement since all be was carrying was his rifle and she could see no transportation. She told him that he was to turn around and walk to the gate and leave the way he had come. He took a step towards her and asked her if he could at least have his rifle back. Morgan told him no, that that was the admission price to crossing her gate.

Again he took a step forward begging for her to let him have his rifle and to sleep in her barn for just one night. Again Morgan told him to turn around and go back the way he came. Just as she thought he was going to do as she asked, he reached as fast as she had ever seen a man move and grabbed the barrel of her rifle pulling it out of her hands. Wolf started to pounce and he told her to call him off or he would kill him then and there. Morgan quickly called Wolf back and the two of them stood watching the man to see what he really wanted. He told her that he wanted her to take him into the cabin because he intended to stay the night with her and tomorrow he would hunt on her land. He said that it was wrong for a woman to be living alone and that she needed a man with her. He stank of whiskey and she could tell by the way he looked at her what he was going to do once he got her inside. She said no and he said either do it or I'll kill your wolf. Slowly, Morgan began to turn around and motioned Wolf to go in front of her. The man let down his guard as he thought she had given up but when he lowered the rifle just a few inches she quickly drew her hand gun from her belt and shot him in the heart. He looked at her as if he couldn't believe what had just happened to him and fell to his knees and then on his face. She walked over and reached down and felt for a pulse. There wasn't one.

She told Wolf to go to the door and she backed away from the man and went with Wolf into the cabin and immediately keyed the radio for Willa. When Willa answered, Morgan asked to speak to Mr. Stone. Mr. Stone got on the radio and she told him that she needed him to bring the sheriff and come as quickly as possible. Mr. Stone knowing Morgan as he did didn't waste time asking questions. He said that he was on the way and gave the radio back to Willa. Willa's voice was shaking when she asked what had happened and Morgan told her that she was fine but that there had been an intruder and she needed the sheriff. She didn't want to tell Willa that she had killed the man. Morgan locked Wolf in the cabin and went back out and covered the body with a blanket and then stood in the cold to wait for the Sheriff. She didn't know what was going to happen since she nor Wolf had a mark on them and the man looked presentable. When the Sheriff and Mr. Stone arrived, Morgan was standing in the front over the body of the man. She told the Sheriff what had happened and gave him her handgun. She pointed to where her rifle had fallen and to where his rifle was on the ground. She had not touched either rifle or the man, only covering him. The Sheriff lifted to cover off of his face and looked up at Morgan. He told her that an ambulance was on the way to pick up the body and take into town to the morgue. He then suggested that they go inside and talk since it was so blamed cold outside.

On entering the cabin, Morgan had to motion for Wolf to stop, as he had never see the Sheriff before. She went through the normal ritual of introducing someone to Wolf and after he accepted the Sheriffs presence and lay down on his blanket the three of them sat at the table. Morgan poured coffee for all three and sat down putting her hands on the table in front of her and looking the Sheriff in the eye. The first thing he told her was that she should relax as he recognized the man outside. He was on the run from another state where he was wanted for assault and rape and there was no evidence that anything happened other than what Morgan had said. He told her than he had known Mr. Stone all of their lives and that if he vouched for someone that was all he needed to know. They could hear the ambulance coming down the road and the Sheriff and Mr. Stone went outside telling Morgan to stay and they would be back. It was only a few minutes before the ambulance once again went down the drive headed back to town and the two men came back into the cabin. Sitting at the table the Sheriff told her that procedure demanded that he call for a grand jury to hear the evidence but that he wasn't going to take her in to town. He would talk to the judge and she would not have to pay a bond, as he was sure she would be no billed. Actually, she had done them all a favor by getting this savage off of the streets. The talked a few more minutes and then the two men left to go back to town. Mr. Stone stopped at the door and put his arm around Morgan and squeezed her shoulder asking if she would be all right. She assured him that she would and asked him to tell Willa that she would talk to her in the morning. With that, the two men left and Willa went to the window to watch them drive away. She knew that Mr. Stone would lock the gate behind him so she turned and checked all of the doors, poured herself a cup of tea and went to sit on the couch by the stove. She looked down at Wolf and once again gave thanks to her ancestors and her Lord. Shortly she got up and motioning to Wolf went into the bedroom and went to sleep.

SECTION 10

Morgan was no billed by the grand jury as it was definitely ruled self-defense. She had taken a human life and she knew that what she had done was wrong but had she not done it, she and Wolf would most likely be dead now. She tried to put it behind her and get on with the business of living.

The winter moved on with several more snowstorms but nothing as severe as before. Morgan rode Horse and went to town and Wolf was back to his old habit of staying gone all-day and coming back at night. Morgan read and planned for spring. She had an idea that she wanted to build another cabin further up in the hills closer to the pond so that she could watch the animals feed from a better vantage point. From where she was now, it was too far away to see very well. She sat and drew out plans for a very simple but beautiful cabin. It would have a large kitchen with all of the comforts that she had now but there would be a table in front of the bay window that looked out over the pond. Not too close but close enough to see the animals when they came. The great room would have a wood burning stove and windows on both sides, again so that she could see the beauty around her. She would again have only one bedroom and bath but there would be windows in the bedroom again so that she had the outdoors with in sight. The only problem was what she should do with the cabin she had now. She didn't want to tear it down or move it so she just left it alone knowing that an answer would come along.

As spring began to show her face, Morgan went into town and got in touch with the carpenter who had done some work for her last year. She told him what she wanted to do and he said that it would be no problem and he could start clearing the land right away. She also wanted him to make a permanent sidewalk for Willa's chair from the road to the porch on the old cabin. He said that he would get right to work and he didn't think it would take long since she was keeping things pretty simple. So, the deal was made and Morgan was excited to be moving to a place higher on her land where she could see more from her windows. She went over to the hardware store to tell Willa and Mr. Stone but when she got there the store had the "closed" sign on the door and the lights were out. Morgan knocked and finally Mr. Stone came and unlocked the door and let her in. They went back to the back room and sat down at the table and Willa poured them all some tea. Morgan hesitated to be pushy but she was concerned over why the store was closed on a weekday morning.

Mr. Stone told her that he and Willa had decided to retire. He said that he had a good offer to buy the store and they were going to take it as he was tired of working inside all day and Willa wanted to be in a house, not in back rooms in a store. They were still young enough to do what they wished but too old to work all day every day without a break or any help. He said that all they had to do was to find a house that they could buy or rent because they didn't want to leave the area, as this was their home. Morgan was so excited she couldn't contain herself. She blurted out her plans for a new and smaller cabin further up on her land and begged them to move out and live in the larger cabin she was in now. She told them that she wanted them to be out with her so badly and that she could help them when they needed it as they could do the same for her. Mr. Stone looked at Willa and she was smiling with tears running down her soft cheeks. So it was decided. The new owner would let them stay until the new cabin was built but Morgan insisted that they move immediately. They had no real furniture to bring and all that they did have would more than fit in the cabin. She planned on packing some of her things anyway in preparation of her move to her new cabin. So much excitement was all around them it was all they could do not to jump up and down.

Calming down they made their plan. The deal on the store had closed that morning and all that had to be done was to pack up the things that they wanted to move with them and put them in Morgan's truck. Then they would follow her to the cabin in their car. It didn't take long because Morgan was a whirlwind. Willa could only sit and wonder at where she got the energy. By midafternoon, all was loaded and Mr. Stone handed the key over to the new owner, got in his car with Willa and drove away towards his new home. Once they arrived, they got Willa in and settled and Mr. Stone and Morgan emptied the truck and she insisted that he park his car in the garage, as her truck would not mind the cold or the wind. She made a mental note to have a new garage big enough for her truck attached to her new cabin. While they had been unloading, Willa had cooked supper and when they were finished they sat down to eat. Holding hands around the table they thanked the Lord for all of his many blessings. After supper Morgan insisted that she would clean up the kitchen since Willa had cooked and this became the habit until Morgan moved into her new cabin.

When she went to town to buy furniture for her new place to be held until it was ready, she bought a queen sized bed for her old bedroom. She planned on taking her double bed with her to the new cabin and wanted a nice new bed for Willa and Mr. Stone in the bedroom. The carpenters worked diligently on getting the new cabin built. They brought in a road grader and took the existing road on up to the new place. They brought in rock for the new road and Morgan made sure that they remembered to build a ramp for Willa so that she could come from either place at her choosing. As a matter of fact, Morgan had a great idea. She had a stonemason come in and lay a smooth stone-curving sidewalk from Willa's back door to Morgana's back door. All Willa would have to do would be to come out the door and turn to the left and there would be the start of the beautiful stone sidewalk. It was as level as it could be made so that she wouldn't have to push herself up hill. The grade upwards had been made as gradually as was possible and Willa proved herself strong enough to get back and forth on her own.

While all of the building was going on, Morgan was riding Horse and getting the garden ready for planting after the last frost. She also had the carpenters come into the kitchen in the old cabin and make some renovations there as well. They lowered the counter and the sink in the kitchen making it much more manageable for Willa to get around without having to stretch so much. They also enlarged and installed a shower that Willa could roll right into thus getting rid of the problem of the high sided tub. They installed a new counter with a sink low enough for Willa and another sink that would be the right height for Mr. Stone. Thank goodness the doorways were unusually wide so they didn't have to move doors for Willa. She was so pleased with the new arrangements because she could maneuver much better now with things at her own level. Willa and Mr. Stone were still sleeping on the pull out couch in the front room and with three people using the small bathroom it was getting somewhat crowded. There was nothing to be done for it until the new cabin was ready and Mr. Stone spent most of his days outside. It turned out he was a true landscaper and Morgan told him to do as he wished with all of the walkways and cabins. She and Mr. Stone had a private meeting outside one day where he insisted on paying Morgan for the cabin and the land it stood on. She would have none of it. She told him that she had already deeded the cabin and five acres of land to him as a gift and that she would hear no more about it. She told him that she knew that without Willa and him she would not have made it through the winter and it was her gift to herself to do this for them. She wanted them near to her and she knew that it was right. Mr. Stone had no choice but to accept her gift but he assured her that he would take on much of the work around the place because he liked to work and she needed more free time for her garden and her exploring with Horse. They sealed the deal with a handshake and a hug and it was done.

SECTION 11

The progress on the cabin was going at such a rate that Morgan decided to move in before it was completely finished. She asked the carpenter to finish the bedroom and bathroom first as she could take her meals down at the big cabin. As soon as this part of the cabin was complete, Morgan moved her double bed, with the help of the movers that had brought the new furniture. She had her bed and her dresser and chest of drawers along with her chair moved into the new bedroom. She moved all of her toiletries from the old bathroom and stocked the old bathroom with all new towels and linens for Willa. She had also bought new linens and towels for herself. The wood stove in her bedroom was lighted, and it drew perfectly, so when supper was finished that night, she visited for a short time and then walked with Wolf up to the new cabin.

She and Mr. Stone had the new queen size bed moved into the bedroom and she made it up and put in a brand new dresser and chest of drawers for Willa. She also bought her a chaise lounge that she positioned so that Willa could either read or just rest and look out the window. Willa was absolutely thrilled at the new things and the way that Morgan had laid the room out. She said that she would have done it exactly the same way herself, so all was well.

The first night that Morgan spent in her new house was a little bit strange in that she had to be careful not to trip over the work that was still in progress. The kitchen had been finished as far as the electrical outlets were in place as well as the stove and refrigerator. They were all built in so it hadn't really been any trouble for the builders to work around them. After her first bath in her new home she but on her night dress and robe and went to the kitchen and made a cup of tea. There was nowhere to sit except her bedroom so she took her tea and motioned to Wolf to follow and they went into the bedroom and closed the door so that the heat would stay in. The wood stove in the great room hadn't been lighted yet and it was still cold. She sat in her chair by the stove in her bedroom and Wolf lay on his blankets by the stove. She thanked her ancestors and her Lord and finishing her tea climbed into bed, turned out the light and was asleep immediately.

She woke at dawn and looked down at the old cabin. Seeing lights on she dressed and made herself some coffee and she and Wolf walked down to the Stone's and she knocked on the back door. Mr. Stone opened it immediately and told her that she was never to knock again. She was to continue to come and go as she always had and unless she wanted it different so would they. Morgan thanked him and that was settled. Willa sang out a good morning and Morgan sat at the bar and visited with Willa while she made blueberry pancakes and bacon for breakfast. When all was ready, they sat at the table together and held hands to thank the Lord for all of his blessings. The breakfast was delicious and as soon as Morgan had cleaned the kitchen they could hear the trucks coming up the road for another days work. Mr. Stone and Morgan had made the decision together to disarm the alarm while the construction was going on and to leave the gate open. They both felt that it would be safe since there were so many people about on the property and they were right. So, the day began and there was activity everywhere.

Willa was in the cabin re-arranging and setting things to her taste and her ease of getting here she needed to be. Mr. Stone was in the ham with Horse as the two of them had hit it off so well. Mr. Stone usually took care of Horse everyday now that they lived on the place and he loved doing it. Morgan was up at the new house in the bedroom putting it to rights and Wolf was out on his travels for the day. After being inside for the morning, Morgan wanted to work outside so she went to the shed and got her tiller and decided to till the garden and get it ready for planting. Yes, she knew that it was a bit early but it wouldn't matter if it had to be done again as the soil was rich and the more that it was loosened the better it would be for planting. She had lost herself in thought when she beard the truck leaving for the day and she waved as they drove down the road. She put the tiller up and went inside Willa's and washed up. Willa had made a wonderful meal of pork chops and baked sweet potatoes with yellow squash and fresh baked bread. They had a salad and an apple pie for desert. The conversation around the table flowed easily and it was as if they had been a family of three forever. After cleaning up the kitchen,

Morgan sat with them for a while and then excused herself and taking Wolf walked up to her place to get ready for the night.

She went in the back door and was amazed at the amount of work completed in one day. The kitchen was totally finished. All she had to do was stock it and she could cook her own meals if she felt like it. The wood stove had been installed in the great room and lighted. The room was warm and cozy and the hardwood floors just shined in the glow of the fire. The carpenter had left her a note and said that she could call tomorrow and have her furniture delivered, as the rest of the work would be mainly on the outside. She walked around running her hand over the smooth counters and looking at her new home. The great room was big enough for almost anything and the kitchen flowed into the rest of the room just right. She was so anxious to set up her dining table in front of the big bay window that she wished she had it with her now. But, tomorrow would be soon enough. Morgan was delighted with everything. She had her great room and her kitchen all together as one big area. A door wide enough for Willa should she need to get in separated her bedroom and bath. She had a large pantry in the kitchen so she didn't need a root cellar because the one at the big house would be fine for all of them. The carpenters had built her a large enough garage so that she could park her truck inside without any trouble at all. She gave up on the idea of another shed as Mr. Stone said they had no need for two and he was, as usual right. Morgan didn't have many clothes therefore she didn't need a huge closet but she did have a very nice closet in her bedroom as well as a closet off of the utility room for wet things to dry. The utility room also held a clothes washer and dryer, as she didn't intend to be running back and forth to the big house to do her laundry. She bathed and readied for bed anxious for the morning so that she could get her furniture delivered. Mr. Stone had told Morgan that he would need to install a telephone because of Willa. If something were to happen to her, he would need to get help quickly and they couldn't rely on the two-way radios. Of course Morgan agreed, as she loved Willa as she would her own Mother. They could still use the two-way radios to communicate back and forth between the two homes. Now Morgan was happy that there was a phone because she could call first thing in the morning and have her furniture delivered.

Upon waking the next morning, Morgan made herself some coffee and while dressing for the day looked down at the big house. The lights were on so she keyed the radio and asked if she could bring anything down with her for breakfast. Mr. Stone answered and laughed. He said that

MORGAN

no, she couldn't bring anything except herself because Willa was trying to kill him with food. Such a wonderful way to start a day with so much laughter. Morgan and Wolf headed down to the big house and walked in to the aroma of cinnamon. Willa had made fresh homemade cinnamon rolls to go with scrambled eggs and ham. Morgan said that if she kept this up she was going to have to buy new clothes for all of the weight she would gain. Naturally Willa said nonsense. A person that was as active as Morgan needed to start the day with a healthy meal.

After eating, Morgan's face turned bright red when she asked if she might use their telephone to call for her furniture. Mr. Stone all but fell out of his chair he was laughing so hard. The one person who didn't want a phone was the first to use it. The furniture store promised that her furniture would be there by noon and that was settled. Mr. Stone left to go see to Horse and Wolf had already left for his daily jaunt. Morgan and Willa sat at the table and talked after the kitchen was cleaned. It was so comforting to both women to have each other to talk to and to know that they weren't alone if trouble came again as it surely would. That is what life was all about. Getting through the bad times made you enjoy the good times even more. They sat for longer than normal drinking their tea and enjoying each other.

Finally, Morgan got up and said she had to get a move on, as the furniture would be there soon. Willa promised to come up after the delivery truck left so that she could see all of the new things. Morgan ran back up the stone sidewalk to her little house and the carpenters were busy at work on the outside. She stopped and thanked them for the wonderful work they had done and apologized to them for the push for speed. They all told her that they understood and they were glad to do it as Mr. Stone was a good friend to them all having owned the hardware store for so long. There wasn't anybody in town that didn't just love the Stone's and they were so grateful that they had Morgan to see to them as they entered their retirement. She laughed and said it would probably be the other way around as she was the one who needed looking after.

Hearing a truck she turned and jumped up and down, as it was her furniture being delivered. The movers backed the truck up to the door and began to unload. The first item off of the truck was her precious dining table for in front of the big bay window. It was made of Birdseye maple and had four matching chairs. It was surely a beautiful piece of furniture. Next, they brought in the couch and easy chairs and small tables and rugs. They brought in lamps and cartons packed with paintings and pillows and throws. It didn't take any time at all and they were gone. The very next minute, Willa came through the door and just stared in joy at the beautiful things Morgan had bought. The colors were Morgan's colors. Turquoise, aqua, navies all were blue. She had burgundy and gray throws and pillows and dark green and blue rugs to scatter on the hardwood floors. Between the two women they had the house put together before dinnertime but they were both tired to the bone. Morgan walked back down to the big house with Willa and said she was just too tired to eat. Mr. Stone had made some sandwiches while they were working and he made her take a sandwich back with her in case she wanted it for later. Thanking him and Willa for all of their help, Morgan said goodnight and walked back to her new home. Along the way, Wolf joined her and they went in the door together.

Morgan took her bath and went to bed. She was too tired to eat, as it had been a long exhausting day. She looked down at the big house and all the lights were off so she knew that Willa was in bed too. Wolf was in his blankets by the stove and Morgan fell asleep after thanking her ancestors and her Lord for all of her blessings.

Morgan woke early the next morning and after letting Wolf out made her coffee and breakfast and sat at her new table watching the deer come to the pond to drink. The fawn had grown up during the winter and it looked as if the doe was going to have another baby in a short period of time. What fun to watch them grow on her land?

She looked down at the big house and could see that Mr. Stone was already out with Horse. She hoped that Willa was still resting but she no sooner had the thought than Willa rolled out of the house and into the shed. Laughing, Morgan got up and cleared her dishes. After cleaning up the kitchen she went through her new place moving things from here to there and making it her own. She was so very pleased with her new "hideout" and even more pleased that the Stones were nearby. All of the work had been completed and she and Mr. Stone and relocked and armed the gate as there was no reason for any unannounced company. Everyone knew that if they wanted to visit the Stone's or Morgan they had to call Mr. Stone tint. She still had the peace and quiet that she lived for and yet she had the convenience of communication right down the road. Mr. Stone had talked at length with Morgan about his survival skills and his ability to shoot. He had been to war and was completely capable of taking care of anything that might arise. With he and Morgan together there would be nothing that could hurt any of them.

Morgan dressed and walked down to the big house to see Willa for a moment before working in the garden. After a short visit, she got to work as it wouldn't be long before they could begin to plant. They already had the starts ready in the shed so as soon as the last frost they would be ready to put them into the ground. She tilled more natural fertilizer into the soil today and it was as fine and clear of rocks as she had ever seen. She didn't stop for lunch but worked right through until she was finished. She put the tools back in the shed and Willa stuck her head out the door and told her to go take her bath and then come down for dinner. Willa said she had cooked a special dinner to celebrate their new homes together. Morgan smiled and nodded and off she went. Shortly, she was back and walked into the kitchen to see what smelled so good because she was starving. Willa had been cooking a huge roast in the crock-pot since five that morning. She cooked it with rosemary, garlic, soy sauce and water and it was so tender it melted in your mouth. There were baby carrots and new potatoes with green beans. There were homemade biscuits with honey and a tossed green salad with fresh tomatoes. Morgan had no idea where Willa had gotten fresh tomatoes and didn't even ask. There was gravy and pickled green tomatoes for relish. For desert, there was a homemade lemon meringue pie. Morgan looked at all the food and sat right down. After saying grace, the three friends ate together and talked about their day. It was a delicious meal and they were all so full that they could barely move. Mr. Stone and Morgan cleared the table and did the dishes and each took a cup of tea and went to sit by the stove in the great room. They sat in silence, as they were just too full and too tired to talk. After a short while, Morgan got up and thanked Willa for the wonderful meal. She told Mr. Stone she would see him first thing in the morning as he had plans for adding on to the barn that they were going to discuss. She leaned down and gave Willa a hug and told her good night. Mr. Stone walked her to the back door and when he opened it Wolf was waiting to walk Morgan home. The two of the walked up the stone sidewalk and into the new cabin together as they had many a night before. Morgan changed into her nightdress and her warm robe and slippers and went to the kitchen for a cup of tea. She looked down at the big house and was pleased to see the lights still on. That meant that Willa and Mr. Stone were sitting by the fire talking to each other and that made Morgan happy.

She sat for a while on the couch with Wolf in his blankets nearby and knew that everything she had done had been right. She didn't know how she knew, she just did. She motioned for Wolf to come to her, and with her hand on his head, she thanked her ancestors and her Lord for all their many blessings. With that, she and Wolf walked into the bedroom and she climbed into her bed and Wolf climbed into his blankets. Morgan turned out the light and signed with peacefulness in her heart that she had never had before.

Yes, she had done everything right. She didn't know how she knew, she just did.

www.ingramcontent.com/pod-product-compliance
Lightning Source LLC
LaVergne TN
LVHW041548060526
838200LV00037B/1196